THE STORY OF
King
LEAR

SAVE THE STORY

Melania G. Mazzucco

ILLUSTRATED BY EMANUELA ORCIARI

Translated by Virginia Jewiss

PUSHKIN CHILDREN'S BOOKS

Pushkin Children's Books
71–75 Shelton Street
London WC2H 9JQ

The Story of King Lear first published in Italian as
La storia di Re Lear
© 2011 Gruppo Editoriale L'Espresso S.p.A
and © 2011 Melania G. Mazzucco. All rights reserved.

This edition published by Pushkin Children's Books in 2014

ISBN 978 1 782690 20 7

Set in Garamond Premier Pro by Tetragon, London

Printed and bound in Italy by Printer Trento SRL
on Munken Print Cream 115gsm

www.pushkinchildrens.com

THE
STORY OF
King
LEAR

One

In the 3,150th year after the creation of the world, centuries after the mighty city of Troy was reduced to ruins, in a faraway land in the North Sea, there lived a king. His name was Lear.

Lear's life had been a happy one. He had conquered all the lands that bordered his. Together they formed an island called Britain, a land green with meadows and rich with water, sheep and fog. Lear had been strong, brave and passionate. He knew how to fight and how to love, how to ride on horseback, how to mete out death on the battlefield and in court, how to punish those who rebelled, and how to reward those who yielded. He had gold and silver and bronze, palaces and castles, dogs and servants—so many that he couldn't even count them. His word was law. But then he grew old. Because even a king is mortal.

The old king grew sad and tired. He was tired of everything—of making war, of ruling, of killing and of punishing. He was tired of himself, too. But a king can't stop being king.

He had already done everything. Only now he didn't know how to do it like before. His eyes grew dim, his ears grew deaf, his legs grew weak, his strength faded.

It was exhausting being king. Now he preferred his dogs, his sweet youngest daughter and his Fool to his ministers and courtiers.

One day the sun disappeared from the sky and the heavens grew dark.

One night the moon disappeared from the sky and everything went black.

Nature was going mad—surely this was a sign from the gods. The priest recognized the prophecy: if night falls at noon and the sky empties out, it means that the world will soon turn upside down. Fathers will disown their children, and children will disown their fathers. Friendships will be severed, and there will be strife, war and violence. The rich will become poor, and fools will become kings.

The King scratched his white beard and pointed out that it's not the stars, the sun or the moon that cause wars and strife and hatred—in other words, it's not evil that causes these things. The cause of

wars and strife and hatred is man, said the King, and anyway, he didn't believe in prophecies. "If the world really did turn upside down," said the King, "the old would grow young and the young would grow old."

The prudent priest counselled him to make sacrifices to the gods so that the prophecy would not come true. Lear ignored him.

And nothing happened. Lear was still king, the rich grew even richer, his youngest daughter was still a girl, and his Fool was still a fool. And not only did the King not become young again, he grew older still.

"What is nature?" he asked the priest.

And the priest responded that nature is what is. What has always been and what always will be.

"What is a king?" he asked the priest.

The priest responded that a king is the favourite of the gods, he who has always been and will always be king.

"What makes a king a king?" he asked the priest.

And the priest babbled confusedly that a king is a king, and nothing is needed to make him one.

So King Lear replied that he would remove the crown from his head and relinquish his power.

By which he meant give up the burden of ruling—
of dealing with ministers and taxes, riches and lands,
the army, the people, all the things that weighed on
him—but without stopping being king.

This would give him back his freedom—and, he
hoped, his youth.

The next day was his eightieth birthday.

King Lear, his crown on his head, sat on his
throne, while the others in the hall stood, as a sign of
respect. Everyone was there, summoned from every
corner of the island.

The King had three daughters.

The oldest daughter, Goneril, was married to the
Duke of Scotland.

The middle daughter, Regan, was married to the
Duke of Cornwall.

The youngest daughter, Cordelia,
did not have a husband yet
because she was her father's
favourite. He loved her more
than the other two, and he
preferred to keep her close to
him. The little princess had
many suitors, though. They

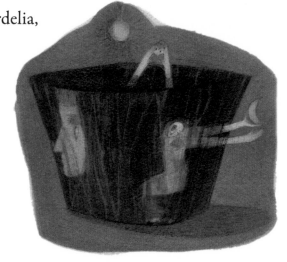

had even come from other lands to ask for her hand. But the King wasn't willing to give her up.

A framed map of Britain stood on an easel in the throne room.

Everyone was wondering what it meant, and why the King had called them all there.

The King removed the crown from his head and placed it on the floor. Everyone's jaw dropped in amazement.

The crown was gold and glittered with a thousand precious gems.

The King said he didn't have much time left, and he didn't want to be responsible for ruling Britain any more. From now on, all he wanted to do was live. The elderly need to know when to step aside, he said. The young must take their place. It's the law of life.

His older daughters exchanged approving glances; it was about time their father realized his moment had passed.

On the King's order, a courtier drew two lines on the map.

One line marked the border of the duchy of Scotland, the other the duchy of Cornwall. That left all the land in the middle.

In other words, the King was dividing his kingdom among his three daughters.

The Duke of Scotland and the Duke of Cornwall stretched their necks, and were pleased to see the King had divided the island into three equal parts.

"But only one of my daughters," the King said, "will become queen after my death."

To decide which one it would be, they each had to answer a question.

"The King's stealing my job. I'm the one who asks riddles," the Fool protested in Cordelia's ear.

"Let's hope it's not too hard a question," Cordelia whispered. She was as timid as a fawn, and didn't know how to talk in front of people.

"How much do you love me?" the King asked Goneril.

His oldest daughter said she loved him more than anyone else in the world, more than her husband, more than her child when one would be born to her, even more than she loved herself. She paused, thinking she had said enough, but then realized she hadn't. She added that her love was so great, there weren't enough numbers to measure it. The kernels of grain in a field can be counted, and so can the rivers and mountains on earth, but not the stars in the sky. Likewise, she said, the love she bore her father was beyond measure.

King Lear was very pleased.

"How much do you love me?" he asked Regan.

His second daughter said she loved him no less than her sister—if anything, even more. But words were not enough to express her love. Words can describe the fury of a storm, the sweetness of sugar, the bitterness of bile, but not the love she bore her father.

King Lear was very pleased.

"How much do you love me?" he asked Cordelia.

His youngest daughter said nothing.

King Lear was chagrined, because little Cordelia was his favourite, and in his heart he knew it was she to whom he wanted to leave his crown. He asked her again.

"How much do you love me?"

His youngest daughter said she loved him as a daughter must love her father. No more, no less.

King Lear's face turned red, then white, then fiery red again.

He had been king for too long. He was drunk on adulation and lies. No one ever told him the truth.

His cheeks puffed with rage and his mouth went dry. I never saw anyone so furious.

Believe me, because I was there.

The King hurled his sceptre at the map.

Britain ripped apart like a tattered rag.

"I alter, revoke and annul what I said," the King roared. "My kingdom shall be divided in two, between my good daughters. Goneril and Regan will share Cordelia's part. Cordelia is no longer my daughter. If only she had never been born! I disown her, delete her, damn her. May I die of hunger on the heath if this ingrate ever receives anything more from me."

"Bring in the hopeful husbands," he commanded.

Two suitors had come all the way from the Continent to ask young Cordelia's hand in marriage. Both were kings—one of Burgundy, the other of France—so King Lear could not refuse them. But since he couldn't bring himself to choose which one to give his daughter to, he had made them wait. The two kings were patient, but they also had to return to their countries, and neither one wanted to leave empty-handed.

"Who wants to be the husband of this wretch?" he asked. "Know that her only dowry is my eternal curse and that she will have nothing but hatred from me."

The King of Burgundy, who had asked for Cordelia's hand thinking to inherit the kingdom of Britain, said he had come to marry a princess, not a beggar, and he left.

The King of France was about to say the same thing as Cordelia wept silently, her eyes lowered. She was the sweetest, most charming creature the King of France had ever seen.

"I will marry you just as you are," he said. "I don't want anything from you, sweet princess. No dowry is worth the beauty of an honest heart, as yours is. My country shall be your home. Come away with me."

"Daddy dear," the Fool whispered, "are you mad?"

"Of course not. *You're* the madman around here," answered the King.

"Whoever grows old without becoming wise is mad," said the Fool. "You're committing a terrible injustice. A wrong question can't help but receive wrong answers. You don't *speak* love, you *do* it. Goneril and Regan lied to you, but Cordelia was sincere, and no one loves you more than she does."

Furious, Lear responded that a king cannot ask a wrong question.

Because a king can't stop being king, and a king is always right.

"I told the truth," the Fool protested. "A madman can only speak the truth."

"I pay you to make me laugh, not to tell you you're right," said the King. And he ordered the Fool to be whipped.

Cordelia said goodbye to Goneril and Regan. "Sisters," she said, "I hope that your hearts match your fine words, and that you will show our father how much you love him. Take good care of him."

"We'll show him, don't you worry," her sisters responded.

The weeping Cordelia followed the King of France aboard a ship that took her far away.

"I had three children, and now I have two," the King said to my father when the foreigners had left. Only friends and relatives remained in the throne room.

"I, on the other hand, used to have one and now I have two," my father said, gesturing to his sons. One of them was setting foot in court for the very first time, and my father wanted to present him to the King.

"But the one who has gained in this affair is me," declared the King.

My father laughed, even though he was shocked by what had happened. He loved Cordelia—as did everyone else—but you have to understand: my father also loved that irascible, white-haired old man. Lear was my father's king. He always had been. And he always would be.

Two

The Earl of Gloucester was a vassal of the Duke of Cornwall and had been King Lear's friend ever since they were young, before they'd grown whiskers on their chins. Gloucester was of noble blood, and rich, though not as rich as Lear. He owned land and horses and a castle. He had a good heart and a weak character. In other words, he was a happy, lucky man.

Gloucester had two sons. The elder, Edgar, was the child of his noble wife. Edgar had grown up in their castle, and was revered by the servants, schooled by tutors and honoured by gentlemen. And he was much loved by his father. Edgar had no experience of the world—all he knew was books. He believed that nature is a ladder on which everyone had been assigned his proper rung. He did not know evil. He believed in the gods. He had a soft heart and was as innocent as an angel. When Lear took off his crown,

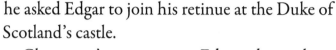

he asked Edgar to join his retinue at the Duke of Scotland's castle.

Gloucester's younger son, Edmund, was the child of a prostitute. He had grown up on the Continent, among foreigners who disdained him because he was born a bastard. His father had sent him away because he reminded him of his sin, which in truth had been a pleasure, though unfit for a man like him. He made Edmund study, to make a place for himself in the world, and after nine years of exile Gloucester decided he should come home. Edmund already knew all there was to know of the world. He believed that nature is a wheel, on which everyone must rise and fall. He did not know goodness. He had a heart of stone. And he was as clever as a demon. He didn't believe in the gods. He saw the King's court for the first time on the day the King removed his crown. His father had presented him to the King, and Edmund meant to profit from the introduction. But then the old dotard renounced his power.

While his brother Edgar served the King without a crown in Scotland, Edmund seethed in his father's castle. The rich nobles avoided him because he was a bastard. The poor folk hated him because he lived like a nobleman even though he came from their world.

One day Edgar would inherit his father's castle and title.

One day Edmund would have to find himself a job. Either become a soldier, a priest, a steward, or a page.

All because his mother wasn't married to the Earl of Gloucester.

So said the laws. Laws are made to oppress the weak.

The Earl of Gloucester was old. Edmund was young.

Peasants died of fever, shepherds of pneumonia, sailors of drowning, prostitutes of fatigue. None of them lived long enough to grow old. But neither fevers nor pneumonia nor shipwrecks nor fatigue touched the Earl of Gloucester.

He was in perfect health.

And anyway, if he were to die, Edmund would inherit nothing.

* * *

Like the sun in the northern lands, which for six months never sets and for six months never rises, the old King without a crown divided his year in two halves.

He decided to live six months with his daughter Goneril and six months with his daughter Regan.

So he settled into her husband the Duke of Scotland's castle with his retinue of a hundred knights.

Since he was no longer king, he had nothing to do but hunt deer, bears and wolves, train his dogs, feast and listen to his Fool's jokes.

It was as if time never passed. It didn't pass for his daughter, either.

Goneril was already regretting their agreement.

Old people are a burden.

House guests are a bother.

And her father was a guest after all. Having already given away his land, his money, his army and his power, he had nothing more to offer—in other words, he was worthless.

House guests start to stink after three days. And many more than that had already passed.

Goneril wanted to get rid of her old, worthless father. But she needed an excuse.

The hundred knights in Lear's train cost a lot and spent a lot. They behaved as if the King were still in charge, whereas now he was merely a guest of his daughter and her husband, the Duke of Scotland.

Lear's Fool was insolent and, what's more, he was devoted to Cordelia, as he never failed to remind everyone. He insulted Goneril. He called her Mummy, because the King, he said, had become her son by putting himself in her hands.

She did not find his jokes funny.

So that was her excuse.

Treat the servant poorly so as to teach his master a lesson, she thought.

She had the Fool whipped.

King Lear was very fond of his Fool. He whipped him too, but he had a right to. That boy belonged to him.

The King got very angry when he found out that Goneril had mistreated something of his.

I think I already mentioned that Lear was touchy and bad-tempered.

He protested, demanded explanations from his daughter, expected apologies.

Goneril laughed. This was *her* house, she said, yet Lear's hundred vulgar and dissolute knights had turned it into a tavern, which was intolerable. So she informed her father that she had dismissed fifty of his knights.

Lear objected that his knights were gentlemen and, regardless, fifty knights were not enough because a king needs a large retinue to remind his subjects of his dignity.

Goneril said that he no longer had subjects since he no longer governed, and that fifty knights were more than someone who was retired needed.

"I am your father," Lear reminded her. "My blood runs in your veins, I gave you my kingdom, my money and everything I had, and you repay me by stealing the little I have left?"

"My dear father, you may stay as long as you like," Goneril repeated, "but in my house I make the laws, and your men must respect them."

The King's oldest daughter was proud, fierce and arrogant.

King Lear's face turned red, then white, then fiery red again.

His cheeks puffed with rage and his mouth went dry.

"You are no longer my daughter," he roared. "I disown you, delete you, damn you."

Goneril was afraid of actions but not of words, so she merely shrugged her shoulders.

"May your bones turn to dust," Lear shouted. "May your womb rot, may it be devoured by worms! May the gods make you as sterile as a stone, so that you never give birth to an heir! And if they do grant you a child, may he be a monster of ingratitude, malice and cruelty, so that you will understand what it means to be disowned by your own flesh and blood."

The Duke of Scotland, who had just arrived, didn't understand what the fuss was about. Upon hearing those dreadful words that, in the end, concerned his future as well, he asked what in the world had happened, and why the King had turned so against his wife. Scotland was meek of heart and faithful by nature.

But Goneril didn't explain a thing, and Lear wouldn't even deign to look at him.

"I had two children, and now I only have one," he concluded. "Regan will know how to treat her father."

"Yes, I think she will," Goneril responded with a smile.

But she wasn't really so sure, so she called her
faithful steward, had him saddle her swiftest horses,
and sent him off in great haste along the road heading
south.

"Let's go, let's leave this wolf's den," Lear yelled
to his knights. "We'll meet up at the Duke of
Cornwall's castle."
    And so it was that Edgar wrote a letter to Edmund
to let him know that the King's retinue would be
stopping at Gloucester's castle along the way to
Cornwall, and to ask their father to be there,
because he hoped to see him.
        Edmund threw the letter on the fire.

Three

The Earl of Gloucester was flustered. Hosting a king, even one without a crown, wasn't an everyday occurrence.

The King's messengers informed him that Lear would arrive with fifty knights, so he needed to gather hay for the horses, ready the stalls, roast some sheep, set tables and welcome the guests. As if this were not enough, the Duke of Cornwall and his wife Regan had already showed up at the castle unannounced, and had ordered him not to reveal their presence to the King because they had no desire to speak with him, which seemed to the good Earl of Gloucester a gesture of incredible impoliteness.

What's more, he had heard word that the apparent concord between the dukes was feigned: Cornwall wanted to make war against Scotland and seize all of Britain—but the good Duke of Scotland was reluctant to get involved in a civil war.

In the midst of all this turmoil, Gloucester's beloved son Edgar had disappeared, and his bastard son Edmund had quietly holed himself up in his room in the tower.

The Earl of Gloucester went to see Edmund and found him reading a letter, his eyes wet with tears.

Gloucester asked to read the letter, but Edmund said he preferred he didn't because it would cause him much displeasure, and he would never want to displease his beloved father.

The Earl of Gloucester insisted, and Edmund insisted back.

The Earl of Gloucester commanded, and Edmund relented.

"A good son always obeys his father," Edmund said, "and I want to show you that, despite your prejudices about my birth, I am a good son."

The letter was signed by Edgar.

"Our father is old, we are young," the horrified Earl of Gloucester read. "The law that requires the young to respect their elders, and elders to rule, is contrary to nature. In nature, it's the strongest who commands. The time has come to take our father's place. Kill him and I will give you half of my estate, half of my wealth, half of my name."

"I can't believe my eyes," thundered the Earl of Gloucester. "This is loathsome. Where have I been living until now—on the moon? I never realized what was lurking in my beloved Edgar's heart."

"My good brother could not have written such a thing," Edmund consoled him. "It must be forged."

It was, in fact. Edmund had written it himself.

But alas, the Earl of Gloucester insisted that the letter was Edgar's, for he recognized the handwriting. How distressing, he said. How sad.

His beloved son had deceived him. He'd thought him an angel, but he was really a devil.

"To betray your own blood! To depose your own father! To kill him!"

The Earl of Gloucester's face turned red, then white, then fiery red again.

His cheeks puffed with rage and his mouth went dry.

"I'll disown him," he threatened, "I'll delete him, I'll damn him."

"You're old, my beloved father, so be wise. Don't rush into a decision."

But the Earl of Gloucester had already made up his mind.

"You are my son, Edmund," he said. "Edgar is now a stranger to me. I was wrong to judge you poorly. You are good and respectful, and you love me. You

shall be my heir. Edgar will pay for his betrayal. I banish him from my home and from my lands. If he is found here, let him be killed. Sound the trumpets, alert the guards, spread the word throughout the countryside. May death pursue the heartless Edgar."

Edmund didn't even have to try to appear grieved for his brother's cruel fate, because just then the servants rushed in, looking for the Earl of Gloucester. "Come quickly, my lord," they begged. "There's some serious commotion down in the courtyard."

A platform had been constructed in the courtyard. And on the platform was a pillory. And in the pillory was a man, kneeling like a sheep, a bit in his mouth like a horse, a hat with bells on his head. It was the King's Fool.

"What did he do?" asked the Earl of Gloucester.

"He insulted Goneril's steward," murmured the servants. "By unfortunate coincidence they met on the bridge. The Duchess of Scotland has arrived at the castle. She's in the hall, talking with the Duchess of Cornwall."

A fool who disrespects a nobleman! No one is in their proper place any more. What are the gods up to? The world is truly turning upside down.

Meanwhile King Lear was shouting. He was making threats. I think I already mentioned he was bad-tempered. He wanted to know who it was who had committed such an offence.

Just then Regan, his middle daughter, came out to meet him. "I did," she said to her father. "Your Fool insulted Goneril's steward. He called him a scoundrel, a panderer, a bootlicker."

"My Fool merely spoke the truth."

"The truth!" Regan laughed, "Since when were you interested in the truth?"

"I demand, require and order that my boy be freed," said the King.

"Father," Regan said with a smile, "you're not the one who makes the laws around here. My husband, the Duke of Cornwall, is lord of all, and he has ordered that your Fool pay for his insolence against our sister and her nobleman. But since he is not a vindictive man, he pardons him now."

Cornwall's servants freed the Fool.

King Lear could hardly believe that his middle child could talk like this. Regan had such a mild, gentle character.

"I shall pretend that none of this ever happened, my child. I forgive you," he said. And then he let her know that he would be coming to stay with her earlier than planned, since Goneril, that tiger disguised as a woman, that viper with a forked tongue, had insulted him and he had cursed her.

But Regan defended her sister. She couldn't believe that Goneril was in any way to blame. "You're the one who should ask forgiveness of her for having abused her generosity. You should return to her immediately and stay for the whole time you'd agreed upon. She's here as well. There's still time for you to mend your quarrel."

Lear said that it was too late: Goneril no longer existed for him. Regan was the only child he had left. And that she should make ready her castle, since that was where he was headed.

Regan was alarmed. She said she wasn't ready to host him. And that his retinue was too large, there wasn't room for all of them in Cornwall's castle. And besides, what did he need fifty knights for, anyway? She might possibly allow him twenty-five, but not a single knight more.

"But that wasn't our agreement," said Lear, incredulous.

"Things change," said Regan. "If you want to come and live with us, you're more than welcome, but these are the new rules. Come to think of it, what are you going to do with twenty-five knights? Our servants should be sufficient for you."

"Dismiss the King's knights," Cornwall said to Gloucester. "Let them go in search of adventure, for they are no longer needed."

So Lear realized that his two daughters were in cahoots about seizing the kingdom. And that Regan was made of the same stuff as her sister. They both had hearts of iron.

King Lear's face turned red, then white, then fiery red again.

His cheeks puffed with rage and his mouth went dry.

"I disown you, delete you, damn you," he roared. "May your bones turn to dust, may your womb rot, devoured by worms! May the gods make you as sterile as a stone, so that you never give birth to an heir!"

"Here he goes again," Regan said to her husband. "The same old story. It's amazing how tedious old people are."

"I don't need your castles and your servants, I don't need your charity," Lear said as he headed for the gate. "I don't need anything. It's not the crown that makes a king."

"Where are you going, my lord? Stay here," the dismayed Earl of Gloucester cut in. "It's almost dark, the sky is teeming with clouds, it's already pouring, there'll be a storm tonight."

Ignoring Gloucester, Lear continued to denounce Regan. "You are no longer my daughter," he told her. "I don't have children any more. I don't have anything any more."

"You still have something, Daddy dear," said the Fool, trotting after the King. When he caught up with him, he stuck his Fool's hat on his head.

"A madman's cap? How dare you?" the King said. The Fool was really very insolent.

"You were once a king and now you're a snail, who brings his whole house with him. You used to have everything and now you have nothing. Who's madder than you?" the Fool said.

"Come with me, whoever loves me," Lear said as he went through the gate of Gloucester's castle and set out on the dark road that disappeared into the heath.

His three dogs—Tray, Blanch and Sweetheart—
ran yelping after him.

Lear didn't even turn around to see if anyone else
was following. Because he knew that when a man
falls into disgrace he has no more friends. Of all those
who had been loyal to him when he was rich and
powerful, only one followed after him now. It was
his Fool.

"No one is madder than you, Daddy dear."

Four

In truth, there was someone madder than the King. Edgar, the elegant young nobleman who was supposed to be Earl of Gloucester one day, was reduced to begging for alms in the street and hiding in sheepcotes and chicken coops in order to escape his father's guards, who were searching for him in order to cut off his head.

Barefoot, filthy, smelly, his beard and hair swarming with lice, naked except for a leafy vine wrapped around his waist, Edgar was unrecognizable. He wouldn't even have recognized himself had he looked in a mirror.

But he didn't have a mirror. He didn't have anything. All he had left were his flesh and bones, his head and his heart—which ached as though it had been pierced with a thorn.

He ate stale bread and acorns, and he walked. He didn't know where he was going. One road's as good as another for a vagabond, a madman without a home, without a name.

The weather was awful. It rained cats and dogs. Thunder rattled his bones and lightning lit up the night as if it were day. The wind whirled furiously, hurling into the air everything he encountered on his path—leaves, roof tiles, roots.

In Gloucester's lands there wasn't even a tree to take shelter under, for miles and miles. A tree, mind you! Not even a shrub.

Only meadows soaked with rain, and bogs and swamps where he sunk up to his knees. A heath, like so many on the island of Britain.

In a flash of lightning, Edgar glimpsed a dark spot, a house maybe. Starving, soaking and shivering with cold, he dragged himself towards it.

It was a shepherd's hut, now abandoned, with a peat roof. It stank of goat, of damp straw and animal droppings.

But to Edgar it seemed like a palace. He flung himself inside, covered himself in moss, and fell fast asleep.

The rain had turned to hail. Hailstones as big as hazelnuts bounced off the shoulders and backs of the old man and boy who had strayed off the main road in the dark and were now wandering about in the mud, sinking into the bogs.

"I'm tired," Lear said. "I want a carriage."

"We have no carriage, Daddy dear," said the Fool, "but I can give you my legs."

"I'm getting soaked," said Lear. "I want an umbrella."

"We have no umbrella, Daddy dear," said the Fool, "but I can give you a leaf."

"It's cold," Lear said, "I want a fur cloak."

"We have no fur cloak," said the Fool, "but I can give you one of moss."

"I'm hungry," said Lear, "I want some meat."

"We have no meat, Daddy dear," said the Fool, "but I can give you a stone."

"How do the poor survive?" Lear exclaimed, scratching his head. Bells tinkled. He was still wearing the Fool's hat.

"Like I told you, Daddy, I'm mad, so I can only speak the truth. The poor do the best they can. With their legs, with leaves, with moss and stones."

"And are there many poor people on the island of Britain?" the King asked in astonishment.

"Many?" the Fool replied. "More than there are crickets, more than there are sheep."

"Why didn't anyone tell me this before, when I was king?" Lear asked.

"Because you were king, Daddy," said the Fool.

"And now I'm *your* fool," said Lear bitterly.

He stopped and caressed his faithful dogs' wet fur, unwilling to take one more step.

"Daddy dear," urged the Fool, tugging on the King's sleeve, "just a little farther, come on, there's a shelter over there."

But Lear stopped dead in the middle of the heath, digging in his heels like a donkey who refuses to take another step. The hail pounded his head, and water ran down his face. He looked like a soggy stray dog.

"What do I care about the rain? What do I care about a storm? The sky cannot rain more tears than my eyes have wept, and the winter's chill is nothing compared to the cold in my heart. Nature cannot wound me more than people have. My pain hurts more than this hail does. I was a king, but now I am nothing. I was a father, but now I am childless. What's a storm compared to all this? My mind cracks like the lightning bolts that claw at the night. Wind, sweep me away! Blow me away, like dust."

"Okay, we'll stay here," said the Fool. "Blow harder, winds! Pound harder, hail! Gods, you can do better than this! Give us a real storm! Oh, what fun we'll have!" Blue with cold, the Fool's teeth chattered as he spoke.

"Cordelia, my little princess, my baby, forgive me," said the King as he caressed the Fool's cheek. "You were blameless. You were the most beautiful thing in my life and I cut you off from myself."

"You may have gone mad, Daddy dear," said the Fool, "but you're not blind. Look at me: I'm not who you think I am."

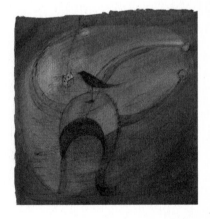

The wind swept the Fool's hat from the King's head.

The Fool dragged Lear towards the shepherd's hut and flung open the door.

Out of the darkness rose a howling beast dressed in leaves.

The Fool howled too.

They both howled in fear.

"Who are you?" Edgar stammered.

"Two madmen dying of cold," stammered the Fool. "And who are you?"

"A man," answered Edgar, falling back on his bed of leaves.

The King stared at him in amazement.

Even this naked, trembling creature was a man.

Edgar crept into the far corner of the hovel. He couldn't believe that this decrepit old man was his powerful godfather, his lord, the man who until very recently had been king. So this is what becomes of man when he loses his power. So little is one worth when he no longer has anything to give to others. But Edgar wasn't up to philosophizing that night.

"Don't disturb my companions," he said, throwing moss on himself.

"What companions?" asked the Fool in astonishment. "I don't see anyone."

"Ruthless demons. Their names are Smulkin, Hobbididence and Flibbertigibbet," Edgar muttered.

"You're mad too," said the Fool, somewhat relieved.

He pushed the beggar aside and arranged the bed of leaves for the King.

The exhausted King ripped off his wet clothes and stood naked.

"What are you doing, Daddy dear?" asked the Fool.

"Becoming a man," said the King, and closed his eyes.

"We can't let the old King set out while a storm is raging, let's go look for him, and bring him some relief," said the Earl of Gloucester to his son Edmund.

"You shouldn't side with him," Edmund warned his father. "You're Cornwall's liege. Cornwall just denied him shelter. Father, if you help the King, you're setting yourself against your lord."

"But he's no longer a king, just a poor old man, defenceless against the power of nature," the Earl of Gloucester stubbornly replied. "We have to be human." And he disappeared into the storm.

* * *

Lear's dogs didn't even bark when Gloucester thrust the lantern into the shepherd's hut because they recognized him. But Gloucester didn't recognize his son-turned-beggar, and the King didn't recognize the Earl of Gloucester—Lear was sound asleep.

"There's a cart here," said the Earl to the Fool, "and a horse waiting for you down by the river. Carry the King to safety. There's no time to lose. They'll come looking for you."

He moved his lantern and caught sight of the naked beast under the straw. That beast had overheard everything. Might he betray them? The Earl of Gloucester had always been disgusted at the sight of poverty. So he decided simply to ignore the beggar, just as he had always done.

"Take our poor King to Dover," he said to the Fool. "Take him to France. His daughter Cordelia is waiting for him, she will take care of him."

"She's forgiven him?" asked Edgar, surprised. "After all the evil he has done to her?"

"She loves him," responded the Earl of Gloucester, astounded that the naked beast knew how to talk. "As a child should love her father."

Five

When the Earl of Gloucester returned to his castle, the guards arrested him.

The Duke of Cornwall had accused him of high treason.

Cornwall wanted to settle the matter as quickly as possible. He was very nervous. Smoke signals rising from hill to hill and from tower to tower alerted him to the fact that the King of France's mighty fleet, under Cordelia's command, was sailing towards the coast of Britain. The enemy ships were crossing the Channel to make war on the Dukes of Scotland and Cornwall and to restore old King Lear to the throne. The Duke of Cornwall had to make peace with his brother-in-law, the Duke of Scotland, and unite their armies to face the invasion.

He ordered Edmund to get ready to depart, as he would have to escort Goneril back to Scotland. Edmund kneeled, and Cornwall placed his sword on his shoulder.

"Today you have lost your father, brave youth," he said. "But in me you have found another one."

"Most grateful," said Edmund with a smile.

In truth, he had no need of another father, having just rid himself of his own.

The Earl of Gloucester could not understand what he had done wrong. He had merely done his duty as a man.

He was led into the courtyard and tied to a chair. He tried to resist, and cried out to Edmund, and couldn't understand why his son didn't rush to help him.

"Shut up, you imbecile," Regan laughed, ripping at his beard.

Let me say that ripping at an old man's beard was the gravest possible insult. It was a way of denying him all respect, of stripping him bare, like a baby.

The Earl of Gloucester groaned, in pain and in shame: he had lost his beard, and would soon be beheaded as a traitor.

But the Duke of Cornwall didn't put him to death. He approached Gloucester and unsheathed his sword.

"Punish the traitor," Regan urged.

And the Duke of Cornwall pierced the Earl of Gloucester's left eye with his sword.

One of Gloucester's servants,
a decrepit old man who until that
moment had stood motionless against
the wall, as if he were a stone gargoyle, leapt
forward and buried his dagger in the Duke of
Cornwall's side. The Duke of Cornwall thrust his
sword in the servant's throat.

"My lord," murmured the Earl of Gloucester's
servant as he fell, "I die happy because my
sacrifice has not been in vain, for you still have
one eye."

"I don't think so," said Regan. And she
grabbed the sword from her husband, who was
writhing on the ground clutching his wound, and
gouged out Gloucester's remaining eye.

She ordered her men to throw the servant's body
on the dung heap.

Blood gushed from Gloucester's empty eye sockets
like water from an overturned jug. He moaned and
invoked Edmund's aid.

"Edmund!" Regan laughed. "He'll never
help you."

And she revealed that it was none other than his
loyal son Edmund who had warned her of his father's

betrayal, and he had been rewarded for his good deed: Edmund, the bastard son, was the new Earl of Gloucester.

Regan's servants untied Gloucester and bandaged his eyes. Gloucester staggered about in shock.

"Monster of ambition and pride, ungrateful heart," lamented the blind Earl of Gloucester. Only now did he see that his bastard son had deceived him, and that Edgar was innocent. Blind, he'd been blind his entire life. And now he had truly lost his sight. There was no way to put things right now. It was too late. Perhaps the good Edgar was dead, and some zealous guard was about to bring him his head. Oh, blind man, oh stupid, blind old man, you well deserve to be punished as a traitor, though not for betraying this tyrannical duke who has blinded you.

As the Earl of Gloucester was being taken away, he brushed up against Edmund, who was accompanying Goneril to say farewell to her sister. But the blind Earl couldn't see his bastard son, and was thrown out of the castle with a kick in the pants.

Regan approached Edmund. "You must leave right away, Edmund," she said, "the country is in danger; there's no time to lose."

Then she knelt over her husband, who was lying pale and incredulous in his own blood.

A noble duke lets himself be stabbed by a base servant. Unheard of. Nothing like this had ever happened on the island of Britain. The world had indeed turned upside down.

"It looks serious," Edmund observed.

Regan knelt over her husband, who had lost consciousness. The Duke of Cornwall was violent, stupid and arrogant. She had never been able to stand him.

"He'll get better, sister," Goneril assured her.

Edmund was young, intelligent and very handsome.

Regan looked at him, and the brand new Earl of Gloucester held her gaze.

"Carry out Cornwall's orders," she said, "do as if you were he. Our troops must prepare for battle. The King of France's troops are about to land, and our sister Cordelia is inciting them to fight and to drive us out of the kingdom."

"At your lady's service," Edmund said. "We shall be victorious."

Six

The Earl of Gloucester—blind, lost and driven from his own land—wandered over the heath, moaning and lamenting his misfortune. I don't know if I've already mentioned this, but he had a good heart and a weak character.

As he stumbled through puddles, falling and pulling himself up again, sobbing and invoking the name of his son Edgar, whom he had unjustly condemned, a mad beggar came to his aid—Edgar.

Edgar wept, too, for his father's cruel fate. But he didn't want to be recognized. The old man had suffered enough already, and he wouldn't have been able to bear knowing that Edgar was in such a miserable state because of him. He preferred to let his father think he was simply a mad beggar willing to guide him wherever he wanted. Edgar, after all, had nowhere else to go.

"Take me to Dover," sobbed the former Earl of Gloucester.

"To Dover?" Edgar was astonished. "Do you mean to join Cordelia, sir?"

But that was the last thing on Gloucester's mind.

"At Dover there's a high cliff at the edge of the sea, and I want to kill myself. Life is an illusion. All is nothing."

"As you wish," Edgar said. "Give me your hand."

And the blind old man gave the mad beggar his hand, without realizing it was really his son's hand.

And together they walked. It was a long way to Dover.

They would stop for the night in chicken coops and pigsties. Even stray dogs avoided them.

They ate stale bread and acorns.

Naked and barefoot, his feet covered in sores, noble Edgar begged on the street, and sometimes passers-by would give him copper coins, but other times they'd spit on him or throw stones.

And Edgar accepted it all—coins, bread, stones and spit—because time was passing and he was changing. He was no longer the stupid, naïve young man he'd been a few months earlier. He was becoming a man. Maturity is everything.

They walked on and on. They crossed heaths, rivers and hills.

The blind man was tired. He couldn't go on.

"When will we get to Dover?" he asked, adjusting the blood-stained bandage that covered his empty eyes.

"We're almost there," Edgar replied. "Can't you smell the sea?"

"No, I don't smell a thing."

"That's strange," Edgar said. "They may have gouged out your eyes, but they didn't cut off your nose. And the air is ripe with the smell of seaweed and guano, of seagulls and salt."

"I'm old," Gloucester said, "my senses are growing dim."

The days passed, but Dover was still a long way away. Edgar liked holding his father's hand as he walked. He liked begging for him, helping him, and he wished their journey would never end.

But when the old man could walk no further, Edgar stopped.

"Come on," Edgar said, "you're just a few steps from the edge of the cliff. If only you could see it! It's a fearful sight. The warships down below, just off the coast, are no bigger than breadcrumbs. And the soldiers look like ants."

Gloucester took heart. He quickened his pace, practically running now. Then he stopped, stretched out his foot on the grass, as if to feel the void below it.

"Now go, poor man," he said to Edgar, letting go of his hand. "I thank you for all you have done for me. May the gods reward you for it."

"The gods?" Edgar replied. "To them, we're as insignificant as ants on the Dover beach, sir. They pay us no mind."

"And you are not as mad as you say," said Gloucester, growing suspicious.

But the beggar had already wandered off.

So Gloucester emptied the air from his lungs, took a deep breath, and let himself fall off the cliff.

But the beggar had deceived him.

There was no cliff, no ravine.

The blind man landed on the grass, just a few feet below the road.

He heard cartwheels creak and harness bells tinkle. He heard seagulls screech.

But he was supposed to be dead.

Do the dead hear? What sounds are there in the netherworld?

After a few minutes, the old man felt his hands. They were still there. He felt his head. It had not been smashed. He felt his face. It was all there—all but his eyes, of course.

"You're alive, stranger," said a man's voice. "You fell from a cloud and you're still in one piece. It's a miracle!"

The old man groped in the direction of the voice, but he couldn't figure out where the speaker was. He thought he recognized the voice, but he wasn't sure. He didn't dare hope. Poor Edgar was probably already dead, some zealous servant was probably bringing his head to the diabolical Edmund. No, it couldn't be Edgar.

"Is the cliff of Dover really that high?" Gloucester stammered.

"Only the stars and the moon are higher," the voice responded. "You could say you rained down from the sky."

"I really fell from such a great height?" the blind man stammered.

"I wouldn't say fall, exactly," said the voice. "The angels must have spread their wings to soften your descent. You must have a good heart."

"Alas, I do not," moaned the Earl of Gloucester. "My beloved son I disowned and banished. Demons accompanied me to this abyss. And yet there is no peace down here either. For I am condemned to live."

Edgar—because you already guessed that the voice the blind man heard was his—helped him to his feet.

"Those demons ran off with the man who led you there, sir," he said. "There are no demons here, only soldiers. But you can't stay here. Three armies are marching on this beach; there will be a battle. It's dangerous, you have to take cover."

"I know your voice, who are you?" Gloucester asked, reaching out his hand to the stranger.

"I'm just a man," Edgar said. "But I am a man."

Seven

Scotland was far away and the journey was long. Goneril was young, and Edmund, the new Earl of Gloucester, even younger. Goneril wanted to be queen, and Edmund wanted power, wealth and glory.

Sparks flew between the King's daughter and Gloucester's bastard son. Love or passion, call it what you will.

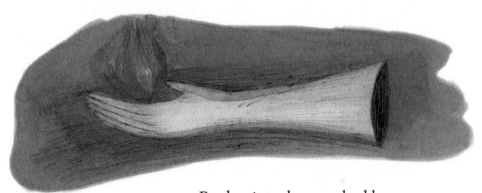

By the time they reached her husband's castle, they were betrothed. Goneril asked him if he was prepared to do everything, truly everything, for her love.

Edmund said yes.

So Goneril told him he had to go back and find the King and kill him. As long as he was alive, the people could always rise up against her.

Edmund promised to do it.

Goneril kissed him and gave him a glove as a token of her love.

When she arrived at her castle, she was astounded that her husband did not come to greet her.

The servants let her know that the Duke of Scotland was very angry with her. Goneril laughed because the Duke of Scotland never got angry. Did I already tell you that he had a meek character?

The Duke of Scotland had received a message from the Duke of Cornwall about ships sailing from France, so he prepared for war. He did so reluctantly, because he preferred dialogue to violence, and the silence of peace to the noise of war.

"I'm going to fight the foreign invaders," he told his wife, "but I shall never lift my sword against the King."

"I never expected you would," Goneril said. "You're a coward. You have a heart of mush and a liver of butter. You're a rabbit, not a valiant warrior like Cornwall."

"Cornwall is dead," said the Duke of Scotland coldly. "His wound got infected, gangrene set in, and they buried him yesterday. Your sister is a widow. Her realm is without a head."

"A widow!" Goneril exclaimed with dismay. So Regan was free! And the handsome Edmund was on his way to her. She had made a huge mistake. She had to stop him!

She leant over the ramparts to see if she could still catch a glimpse of her lover. But he had already vanished.

So Goneril summoned her steward and entrusted him with a secret letter.

"Gallop, run, fly. Catch up with Edmund and when you find him, give him this letter, and give it to him only. Don't open it for any reason in the world. If you do, you're a dead man."

Eight

Cordelia's army was encamped on Dover beach.

Scotland's and Cornwall's armies were encamped in the countryside, inland from the cliff.

In between, in no man's land, roamed two old men, followed close behind by a young peasant wearing a pair of leather shorts. The old men were pushing an empty cart on which a boot was carefully placed. They walked together, supporting one another.

They were both wrecks.

One of them was blind—his eyes had been gouged out.

The other was wearing a crown of nettles, spear grass and wild flowers.

This other man was King Lear, Cordelia's father.

Her soldiers had been searching for him.

Ignoring the blind man and the peasant, they knelt at Lear's feet and asked him to go with them.

Lear pushed the cart with the boot towards them. "Here's the King," he said. "You take him, he stinks of rotting flesh."

The soldiers looked at each other in astonishment while Lear added another flower to his crown. "Patience, old friend," he said to Gloucester, "you can see the world even without eyes, but the crack in my head will never mend."

The soldiers led Lear away and brought him to the Queen of France's tent.

Cordelia knelt at her father's feet and kissed his hands. She burst into tears because the old man's suffering had altered him so. He had become a skeleton with hair, a carcass gnawed by the cold, a lost soul.

"Your suffering is over, father," she said. "Trust me. We shall win this war. You will have your kingdom back. Everything will be like it was before."

"Go to sleep, my boy," Lear said, "you can finally get some rest, I've absorbed all your madness. You are free."

"Don't you recognize me?" Cordelia exclaimed, "It's me, your daughter."

"You are dead," said Lear.

"He's lost his mind," whispered the soldier who had found him. "His reason hides for shame at seeing you again."

"We have to cure him!" Cordelia shouted, and tried to remove the ridiculous crown of wild flowers from her father's head.

But the old man wouldn't let her. He clutched it with his crooked hands, as if it were something precious.

"He'll get better, Your Highness," the doctor said. "Give him a drink to make him drowsy. Let him lay down his guilt in the shadows of sleep."

When Edmund arrived at the Duke of Cornwall's castle, Regan, now a widow, asked him to assume command of her army, and to replace her deceased husband in all things. They set off for Dover together at the head of the troops.

The journey was long.

The widow Regan was young, and Edmund even younger.

Sparks flew between them. Love or passion, call it what you will.

Regan wanted to be queen, Edmund wanted power, wealth and glory.

By the time they reached Dover, they were betrothed.

Regan asked him if he was her sister Goneril's lover, and Edmund said no, because it never pays to tell the truth.

Regan was relieved. Then she asked him if he was prepared to do everything, truly everything, for her love.

Edmund said yes.

Well, then he had to defend their threatened homeland, fight the foreigners who had invaded their lands, and win. Then she would be his.

Edmund promised he would do it.

Regan kissed him and gave him a glove as a token of her love.

Edmund put on his helmet and made his way to the battlefield.

As he galloped off, he asked himself how he would be able to satisfy both sisters. There were two of them and only one of him. But he didn't want to give up either one. Before he had nothing, and now he had too much. The wheel of fortune was carrying him higher and higher, and he didn't want to get off. Power, wealth, glory, love. He wanted it all.

Nine

Goneril's steward had travelled from one end of Britain to the other. He was looking for two things, one easy to find and one difficult. The easy one was the Duke of Cornwall's encampment. The difficult one was a man: the old Earl of Gloucester.

The steward couldn't give his lady's urgent letter to Edmund without first killing the blind old man. For these were his orders.

He wandered along the cliff, which was bustling with soldiers from every corner of the island. Armed to the teeth, they all had seen the blind man with bandaged eyes, but none of them knew where he was hiding.

Goneril's steward was a lucky man. Or unlucky. It depends on your point of view. The fact is that he finally spotted a tree. The only tree on all the fields of Dover.

And in its shade, a young peasant and an old man with bandaged eyes shielded themselves from the scorching sun. The very man he was looking for.

"Good people," he said, in order to draw near without rousing suspicion, "do you know where the Duke of Cornwall's camp is?"

"Why?" asked the young peasant.

Goneril's steward didn't reply, and when he was a sword's thrust away he leapt towards them and tried to run the old man through. The young peasant, who was not a peasant at all, knocked the sword out of his hand and planted a dagger in his heart.

The old man with the bandaged eyes stayed under the tree. He heard a horse neigh, the wind on the grass, a muffled thud and then the buzzing of insects. He didn't understand a thing.

Goneril's steward rolled in the leaves. The peasant searched his pockets and found the letter Goneril had written to Edmund.

"Kill my husband, my love," it said. "And my bed and my kingdom shall be yours."

Trumpets sounded.

The heralds were assembling the troops. The battle was about to begin.

Edgar—because the young peasant was Edgar, of course—told the old man not to move, to stay under the tree, where the arrows wouldn't hurt him. It was too dangerous anywhere else.

He told him to wait there for him, because he had to go—he had a mission to fulfil.

The old man again said he had the impression he'd heard his voice somewhere before.

So Edgar knelt at his father's feet and kissed his hands and told him it was true.

And the Earl of Gloucester recognized his son.

I'll get right to the point. They were reunited, they asked each other's forgiveness, they embraced, they promised to stay together always and for ever. And both of them cried their eyes out.

It's just an expression, because the poor old man didn't have eyes any more. He cried his heart out, let's say.

Gloucester cried so hard, in fact, that as his son raced to the Duke of Scotland's camp to give him the letter that proved his wife's betrayal, the old Earl's heart suddenly stopped beating.

Edgar was already far away when he turned to wave to him one last time.

His dead father was sitting under the tree, a smile
on his lips.

Epilogue

The Earl of Gloucester's bastard son Edmund was born for war. And for glory. If he hadn't been conceived in the bed of a prostitute, if the laws of the land had been different, if rage hadn't poisoned his heart, he would have been a great lord.

He defeated the King of France's troops in battle.

He overran enemy lines, routed their camp, put the French troops to flight and forced their generals to retreat to their ships and sail back to the Continent. Then he entered what was left of France's abandoned camp and took Lear and his daughter Cordelia prisoners.

The old man had slept for days, and when he finally awoke he was being dragged to prison, chains on his feet. But his mind was clear. His madness had left him.

"Don't cry, my child," he said to his daughter, caressing her hair. "We can finally be together."

"I'm not crying," Cordelia said. "I'm happy. I ask for nothing more than to be with you and to live at your side. I love you. I would have followed you even in death. Prison will be our palace."

"We'll be happy," said the King. "We'll have nothing and everything, and we'll laugh at the folly of the powerful, who believe they rule the world when they're nothing more than ants crawling in the dust. We'll finally be free."

Meanwhile, the Duke of Scotland received his victorious ally Edmund without any fanfare.

No trumpets, no flags.

The Duke of Scotland coldly stated that he did not recognize Edmund's victory. In fact, a mysterious knight had appeared, and accused Edmund of high treason.

Stunned, Edmund stared at the stranger.

A knight in a full suit of armour. Only his eyes were visible, gleaming through the slit in his visor.

"I challenge you, you liar, you traitor to dearest affection, adulterer, usurper of thrones," said the mysterious knight. "I have come to avenge the King's humiliation. I have come to redeem your brother's suffering and your father's death. I have come to take your life, which you took from all of them and which you wanted to take from the Duke of Scotland. If I'm lying, prove it."

A cold chill ran down Edmund's spine.

"Don't accept the challenge!" pleaded Regan, who in the meantime had arrived in the camp. "You've won, you will be my husband, the past doesn't matter."

"Kill this impostor, my valorous hero," said Goneril, who in the meantime had arrived in the camp.

Edmund looked first at one, then at the other sister. Both of them loved him.

He couldn't refuse the challenge. He tossed first Goneril's and then Regan's glove at the feet of the mysterious knight, and unsheathed his sword.

Edmund and the mysterious knight duelled under the scorching sun.

Regan fainted and was carried to the Duke of Scotland's tent.

As they duelled, Edmund could hear her moans, which soon became a death rattle.

Regan was dying. Goneril had poisoned her.

Maybe it was because of that death rattle. But the fact is he lowered his guard, and the mysterious warrior buried his sword in the seam of his breastplate, right below his heart. Edmund fell to his knees and Goneril let out a desperate moan.

"Murderous viper, whore's heart," said the Duke of Scotland to his wife.

"Heart of mush," said Goneril to her husband. "You didn't even know how to defend your honour and that of your king." Full of scorn, she entered the tent. Without a second's hesitation, she buried a dagger in her own heart.

"We were supposed to be married today," Edmund said with a smile, as the blood drained from his face, now white as paper. "They'll be my brides in the next world. Shadows amid the shadows, we will be lords of the night."

The unknown warrior removed his helmet.

It was Edgar, Edmund's brother.

Edmund sighed. He was losing consciousness.

"Power, wealth, glory, love," he said. "I had nothing. I wanted everything. Take it all back, it's yours. But I'm not evil by nature or because the stars willed it, and I want my last act on this earth to be my best. Run to the prison, brother. I gave orders that Cordelia be hanged. But her death is pointless

now. Run. If you get there in time, you can still save her."

So Edgar raced to the King's cell.

And there he found them, father and daughter, singing in front of the window, like canaries in a cage, like joyous children.

He freed them and led them to the Duke of Scotland.

The King got his throne back, and upon his death Cordelia became the Queen of Britain.

I know that the Duke of Scotland's descendants and their court historians have circulated another version of the story.

They say that Edgar didn't arrive in time, and that he found Cordelia hanging from the prison bars, murdered by the prison captain. And that the poor old King died of a broken heart as he held her lifeless body in his arms.

And that the wise and gentle Duke of Scotland became the King of Britain, and appointed Edgar his Prime Minister. The Duke of Scotland said that someone as evil as Edmund could not perform a good act, and that the gods had given to Edgar, who was noble of blood and of spirit, the task

of re-establishing justice and of
carrying on.

But the world is much more
complicated than what we're told. Believe me, I
know what I'm saying.

Because I was there.

I'm the one to whom the gods gave the task of
carrying on, of growing up and of recounting it all.

I am Edgar, Earl of Gloucester.

*This book is dedicated
to all my nieces and nephews*

WHERE IS THIS STORY FROM?

The story of King Lear and his three daughters is very, very old. It comes from the mists of time, you could say. To give you an idea: the King lived in the age when Romulus ploughed the furrow on the Palatine Hill, when Rome was still a grazing land for sheep. So just imagine what Britain was like.

Minstrels at court told the story of Lear, and so did grandmothers in front of the fire. Children all over Europe heard the fable: there once was a king who had three daughters...

Time passed. People stopped believing in fables— they only trusted in stories that really happened. So writers remembered to remind us that it was all true.

Their names won't mean a thing to you, but I'll tell you anyway.

Geoffrey of Monmouth wrote the story in Latin. Raphael Holinshed, John Higgins and Edmund Spenser wrote it in English. On the pages of their books, Lear was called Leir or Leire, Cordelia was

Cordeilla, or Cordila, and the Duke of Cornwall was Henuinus. But their characters were always the same. In the end, King Lear would regain his throne (though only for a short time, for he died soon after), and Cordelia would become queen (though only for a short time, because she too was dethroned).

The story belonged to everyone and no one. Whoever wanted to took it and told it in his own way. Some had Cordelia commit suicide in prison, but not until years later, when she was Queen of Britain. Her older sisters were always wicked, but the King never lost his mind, and there were no madmen.

Then an actor named William Shakespeare came along. He wasn't much of an actor, but as a storyteller for the theatre, he was the best. He saw the bad comedy of one of his contemporaries, which was called *The True Chronicle History of King Leir, and his three daughters, Gonorill, Ragan, and Cordella*, and didn't think it worked very well. He read a book by a certain Philip Sidney, who told the story of a blind old man betrayed by his bastard son and saved by his good son. And he liked it. Then he realized that in this barbarous adventure of kings, dukes, princes and princesses, what was missing was the chorus—in other words, a simple person who spoke in a way the audience could relate to, someone who, in other words, spoke the truth: and so he invented the mad Fool with the jester's cap.

Then he combined Lear's and Gloucester's stories, added in the Fool, and rewrote the whole thing.

He told *King Lear* in his own way, and he did it so well that the story became his, and no one else dared tell it any other way.

If anyone wanted to tell the story of King Lear, they had to use Shakespeare's version, with all its absurdities: the storm, the disguises, the madmen, the letters, the poison and the swords.

Since then, there has been an infinity of productions, translations, abridgements and adaptations. Theatre directors broke the rules, cutting things out or moving things around: Lear became a woman, Cordelia became the Fool, Britain a circus, and so on.

But no one dared rewrite the tragic end of *King Lear*, for fear that the ghost of Shakespeare, justifiably indignant, would rise up from his grave and challenge the wicked impostor, piercing him through, just as Edgar does to Edmund.

I wouldn't have dared to try it either, if Edgar hadn't planted the idea in my head.

"I got dragged into this story," he insisted, "and I've been through a whole lot. I've grown old, and they even convinced me that growing up—in other words, gaining experience and understanding human nature—is the point of life. So let me explain my side to the children and their grandchildren.

"Give me back that last battle of the tragedy, which the Duke of Scotland usurped from me. Let me tell how it really went.

"Why does sweet Cordelia have to die? What would be the point in that?

"Do you know it's not true at all? That Shakespeare made it up because he needed a sensational ending, and the actor who played Lear wanted to die on stage with his daughter's dead body in his arms so that the audience would applaud him?

"Cordelia grows up, just as I do. She suffers and struggles, and eventually she becomes a woman. Cordelia is a naïve girl who becomes a queen: that's the point of it all."

To make a long story short, in the end, I let Edgar tell it. This is his story.

Melania G. Mazzucco

THE CREATORS OF THIS BOOK

MELANIA G. MAZZUCCO was born in Rome. In addition to writing, her greatest passions are swimming, flying and travelling. She spends her life telling stories. She wrote her first one, 'The Tiger', in verse, aged seven. It was about a sad tiger in a zoo. She is still writing her latest.

EMANUELA ORCIARI was born in Pesaro. She has won awards with big names, like 'Super Libro 2005' and 'Scarpetta d'Oro'. Yet she says that, in *King Lear*, she has found pretty much the complete story, and a story for everyone.

VIRGINIA JEWISS teaches in the Humanities Program at Yale and directs the university's program in Rome. Her translations include Roberto Saviano's *Gomorrah* and *ZeroZeroZero*, Melania Mazzucco's *Vita* and *Limbo*, and screenplays by Paolo Sorrentino, Matteo Garrone, Gabriele Salvatores, and Margaret Mazzantini and Sergio Castellitto.

SAVE THE STORY is a library of favourite stories from around the world, retold for today's children by some of the best contemporary writers. The stories they retell span cultures (from Ancient Greece to nineteenth-century Russia), time and genres (from comedy and romance to mythology and the realist novel), and they have inspired all manner of artists for many generations.

Save the Story is a mission in book form: saving great stories from oblivion by retelling them for a new, younger generation.

THE HOLDEN SCHOOL (www.scuolaholden.it) was founded in Turin in 1994 with the idea of creating something unique, and is open to students from all over the world. It looks a lot like a huge house with no lack of space, books and coffee. People study something called "storytelling" there—that is, the secret of telling stories in every possible language: literature, film, television, theatre, comics—all of it with the most outlandish results.

This series is dedicated to Achille, Aglaia, Arturo, Clara, Kostas, Olivia, Pietro, Samuele, Sandra, Sebastiano and Sofia.

Just as we all are, children are fascinated by stories. From the earliest age, we love to hear about monsters and heroes, romance and death, disaster and rescue, from every place and time.

In 2013, we created Pushkin Children's Books to share these tales from different languages and cultures with younger readers, and to open the door to the wide, colourful worlds these stories offer.

From picture books and adventure stories to fairy tales and classics, and from fifty-year-old bestsellers to current huge successes abroad, the books on the Pushkin Children's list reflect the very best stories from around the world, for our most discerning readers of all: children.

For more great stories, visit www.pushkinchildrens.com

SAVE THE STORY: THE SERIES

Don Juan by Alessandro Baricco

Cyrano de Bergerac by Stefano Benni

The Nose by Andrea Camilleri

Gulliver by Jonathan Coe

The Betrothed by Umberto Eco

Captain Nemo by Dave Eggers

Gilgamesh by Yiyun Li

King Lear by Melania G. Mazzucco

Antigone by Ali Smith

Crime and Punishment by A. B. Yehoshua